Philipp Winterberg   Nadja Wichmann

KU-622-762

Bin ich klein?
Am I small?

WORLD CHILDREN'S BOOK

AVAILABLE FOR EVERY COUNTRY ON EARTH
IN AT LEAST ONE OFFICIAL LANGUAGE

German (Deutsch)
English (English)

Text (German): Philipp Winterberg
Translation (English): Philipp Winterberg, Sandra Hamer and David Hamer

Text/Publisher: Philipp Winterberg, Münster, www.philippwinterberg.com · Illustrations: Nadja Wichmann · Fonts: Patua One, Noto Sans etc. · Photos: Philipp Winterberg, Lena Hesse etc. · Translation: Heidi Alatalo, Mica Allalouf, Kristel Aquino-Estanislao, Manuel Bernal Márquez, Sanja Bulatović, Jingyi Chen, Aminath Mohamed Didi, Rudolf-Josef Fischer, Renate Glas, Elspeth Grace Hall, Sandra Hamer, Shahzaman Haque, Tania Hoffmann-Fettes, Sabina Hona, Joo Yeon Kang, Şebnem Karakaş, Galina Konstantinovna Zakharova, Chi Le, Kristina Mørch Hendriksen, Alina Omhandoro, Marisa Pereira Paço Pragier, Myat Pyi Phyo, oara Ralaiarijaona, Mialy Razanajatovo, Juga Réka, Saeid Samar, Fiona Sindhikara, Katarina Stock, Iliriana Bisha Tagani, Tshering Tashi, Andreanna Tatsi, Daryna Temerbek, Lobsang Tsering, Laurence Wuillemin etc.
Copyright © 2019 Philipp Winterberg · All rights reserved. No part of this book may be reproduced, stored in a retrieval system, or transmitted by any means without the written permission of the author.

Das ist Tamia.

This is Tamia.

Stimmt!
Genau!

Right!
Exactly!

Tamia ist noch sehr klein.

Tamia is still very small.

Ich?
Klein?

Me?
Small?

Bin ich klein?
Am I small?

**Klein? Du? Du bist kleiner als klein!
Du bist klitzeklein!**

Small? You? You are smaller than
small! You are teeny-weeny!

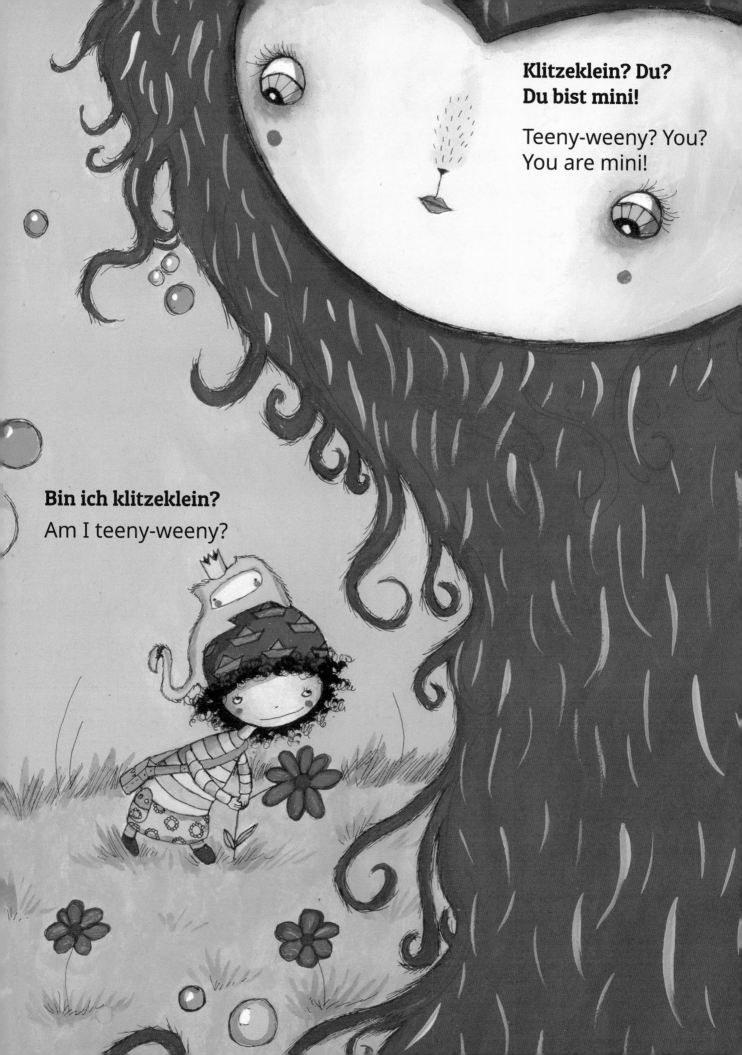

**Klitzeklein? Du?
Du bist mini!**

Teeny-weeny? You?
You are mini!

Bin ich klitzeklein?
Am I teeny-weeny?

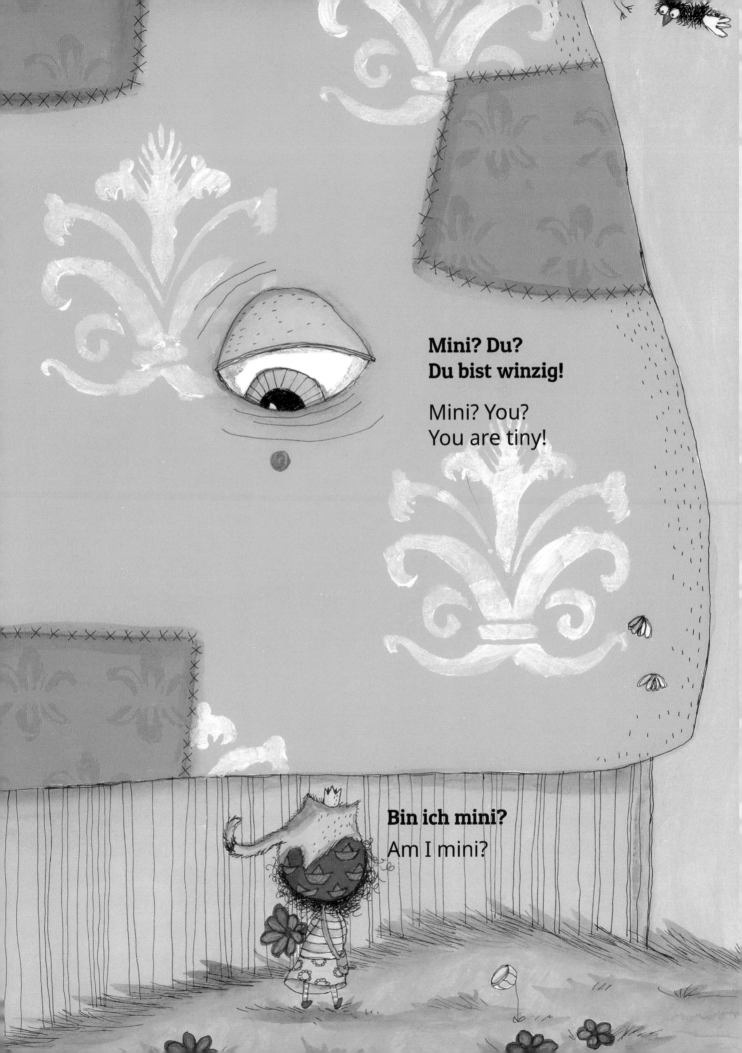

Mini? Du?
Du bist winzig!

Mini? You?
You are tiny!

Bin ich mini?
Am I mini?

Bin ich winzig?

Am I tiny?

Winzig? Du?
Du bist mikroskopisch!

Tiny? You?
You are microscopic!

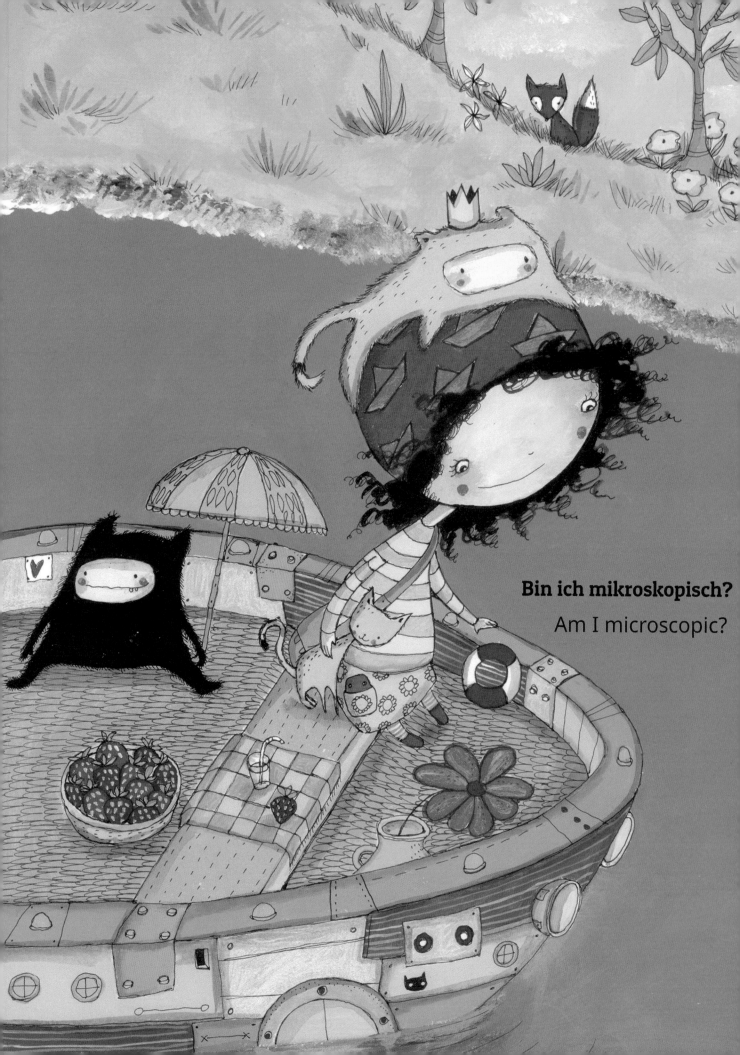

Bin ich mikroskopisch?

Am I microscopic?

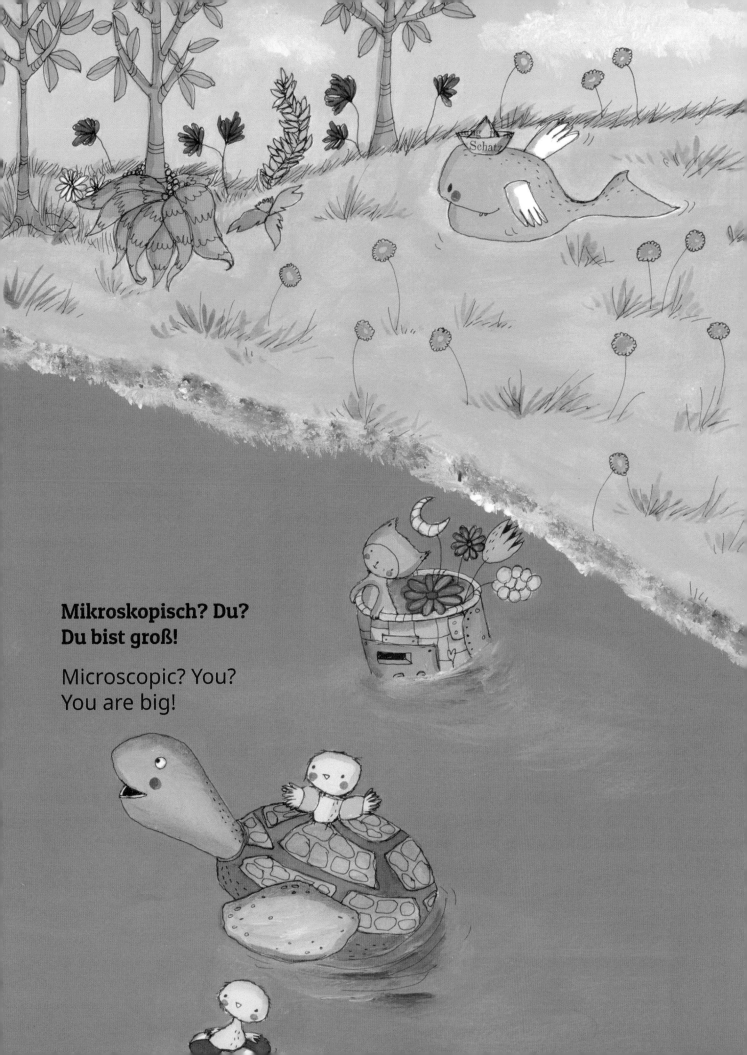

**Mikroskopisch? Du?
Du bist groß!**

Microscopic? You?
You are big!

Bin ich groß?

Am I big?

Groß? Du?
Du bist megagroß!

Big? You?
You are large!

Bin ich megagroß?
Am I large?

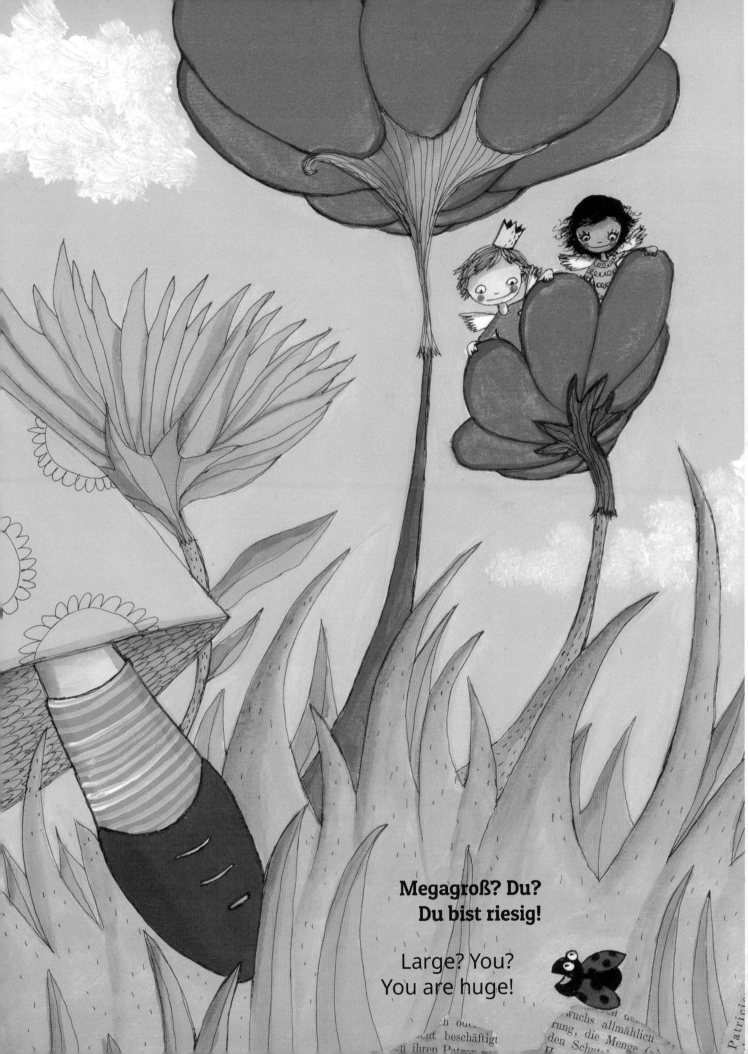

**Megagroß? Du?
Du bist riesig!**

Large? You?
You are huge!

Bin ich riesig?

Am I huge?

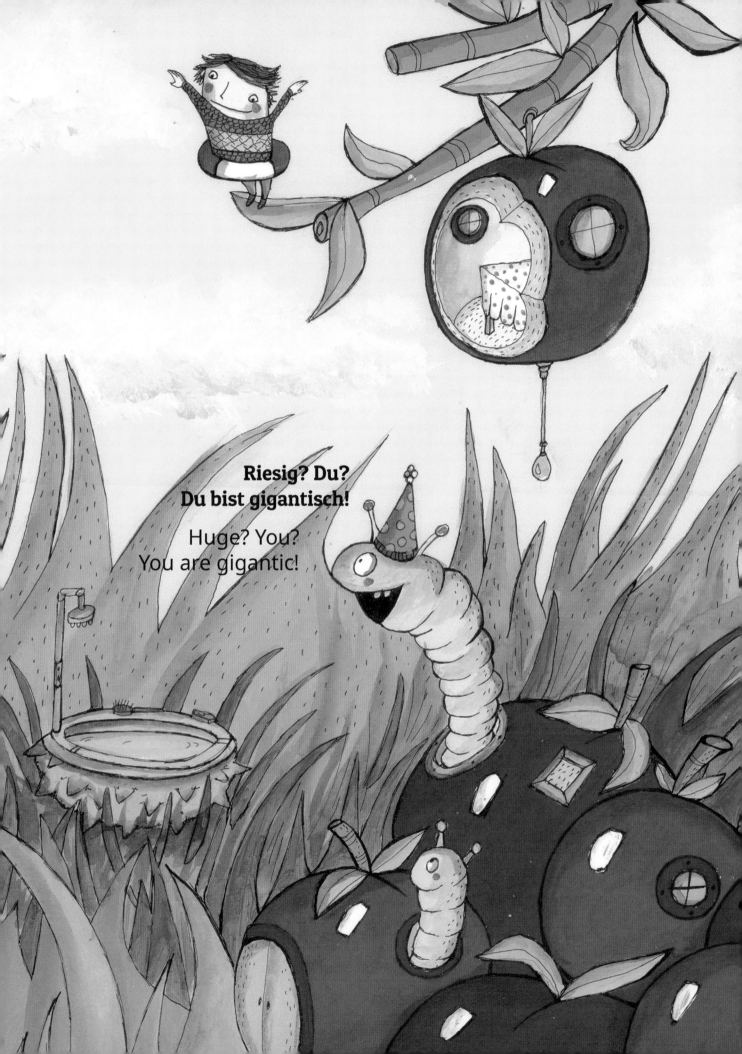

**Riesig? Du?
Du bist gigantisch!**

Huge? You?
You are gigantic!

Moment mal,
ich hab's!
Ich bin alles...

Wait a minute...
I've got it!
I'm everything...

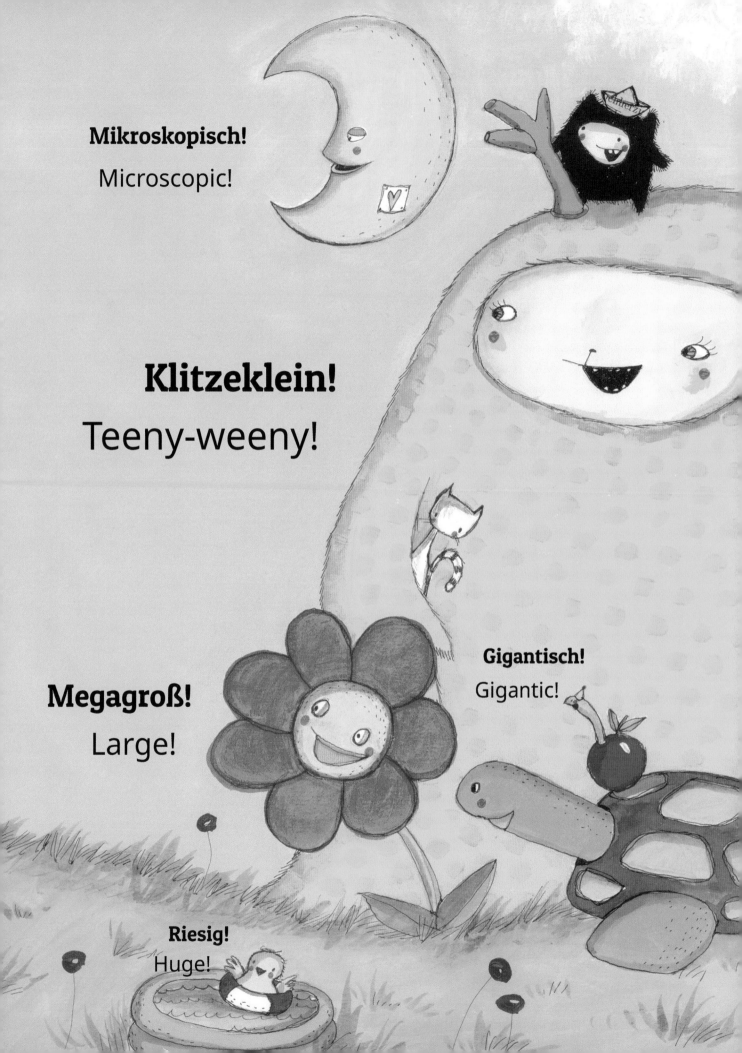

Mikroskopisch!
Microscopic!

Klitzeklein!
Teeny-weeny!

Megagroß!
Large!

Gigantisch!
Gigantic!

Riesig!
Huge!

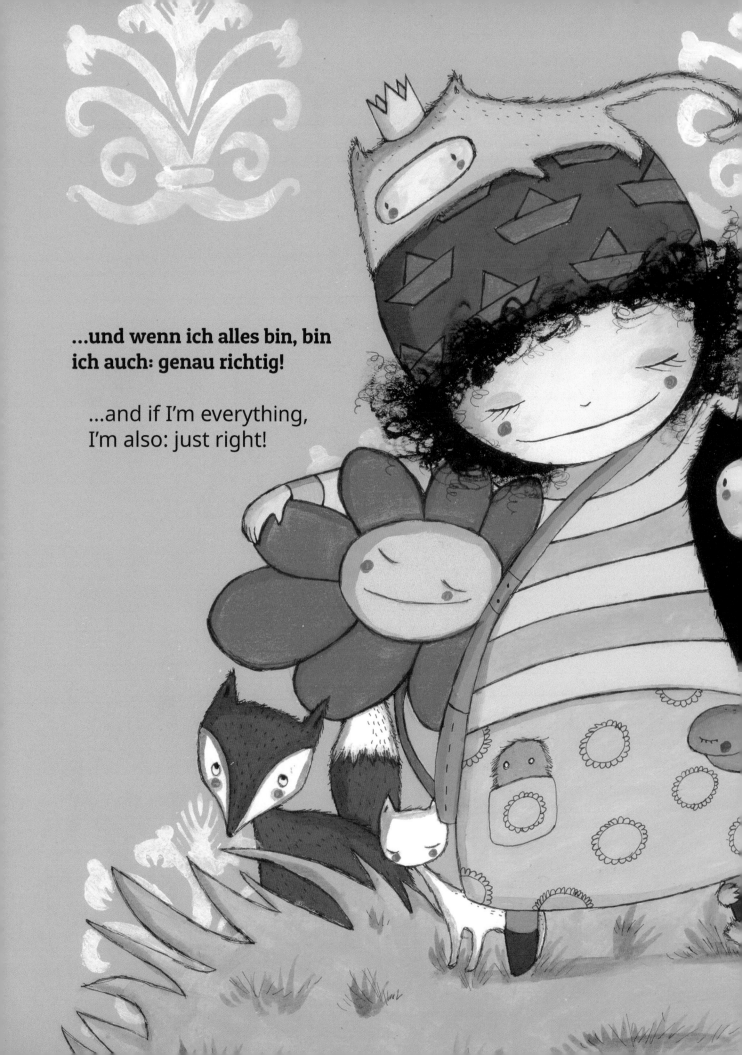

...und wenn ich alles bin, bin ich auch: genau richtig!

...and if I'm everything, I'm also: just right!

Many thanks to all translators!

Mastewal Abera, Tirea Aean, Heidi Alatalo, Mica Allalouf, Rizky Ranny Andayani, Kristel Aquino-Estanislao, Amila Lakshitha Ariyarathna, Senggé Aslan, Andy Ayres, Hroviland Bairhteins, Rajneesh Bhardwaj, Christa Blattmann, Manuel Bernal Márquez, Arrah Brown, Sanja Bulatović, Jingyi Chen, Aminath Mohamed Didi, Tanja Dolinšek, Sumiyabaatar Enkhbaatar, Alejandro Escobedo, Edmund Fairfax, Meliha Fazlic, Rudolf-Josef Fischer, Stephen Gadd, Merrymel George, Renate Glas, Anta Gramm, Sallehuddin Hadi, Tony Hak, Elspeth Grace Hall, David Hamer, Sandra Hamer, Shahzaman Haque, Wiremu Henley, Tania Hoffmann-Fettes, Maryam Holton, Sabina Hona, Petr Hrabe, Tamara Hveisel Hansen, Laura Iglesias Padrón, Liliana Ioan, Akira Ikegami, Farkhod Isaev, Firuz Jumaev, Joo Yeon Kang, Şebnem Karakaş, Galina Konstantinovna Zakharova, Jahan Kos, Anjali Kshirsagar, Irina Kuhtarskih, Dhiraj Kumar, Chi Le, Roy Lin, Niru Liyanaarachchi, Steaphan MacRisnidh, Ruhana Mammadova, Arwa Marwan-Bakr, Mustafa Masoomi, Cheikh M. Mbengue, Majda Mchiche, Kristina Mørch Hendriksen, Ľudmila Košková Nesbit, Henry Kow Nyadiah, Darán Ó Dochartaigh, Fred Mokaya Omangi, Alina Omhandoro, Goran Pavlicevic, Marisa Pereira Paço Pragier, Kheng Piseth, Lusine Poghosyan, Shankar Prasad, Myat Pyi Phyo, H. K. Raghavendra, R. Rajamanickam, Voara Ralaiarijaona, Subramanian Ramaswamy, Mialy Razanajatovo, Juga Réka, María Remírez Balloqui, Dmitriy Rokhlin, Antonella Rosini, Zarina Sadyrbek, Frank Sam, Saeid Samar, Bongiwe Segasa, Aarav Shah, Aaron Crow Simon, Fiona Sindhikara, Bouakeo Sivilay, Katarina Stock, Inara Tabir, Iliriana Bisha Tagani, Pola Taisali, Tshering Tashi, Andreanna Tatsi, Gary Taylor-Raebel, Daryna Temerbek, Lyubomir Tomov, Lobsang Tsering, Mai-Le Timonen Wahlström, Varuwa Vandi, Milica Vranjanac, An Wielockx, Gifty Claresa Wiafe, Isaac Wekesa Wangila, Chor-Tung Wong, Laurence Wuillemin, Yolanda Wu etc.

A World Children's Book for Every Country on the Planet

From Afar to Zulu: The picture book *Am I small?* has been translated into over 100 languages since its publication.

The story by author Philipp Winterberg is available for every country in the world in at least one national language. It is the world's first children's book covering the entire globe.

In *Am I small?* young and old readers alike accompany the girl Tamia on a journey full of wonders. Together they discover that size is relative and that Tamia is just right the way she is. "Enchanting" judges the trade journal *Eselsohr*; "wonderful for bilingual families, and kindergartens," says the *Börsenblatt* and the book review magazine *Kirkus Reviews* kindly compliments "for children who enjoy lingering over pages full of magical creatures and whimsical details [...] told in simple and engaging words and imaginative pictures."

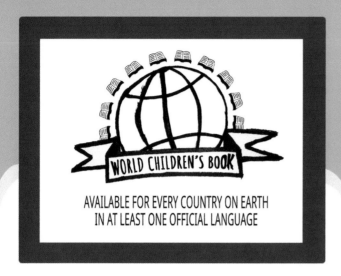

WORLD CHILDREN'S BOOK

AVAILABLE FOR EVERY COUNTRY ON EARTH
IN AT LEAST ONE OFFICIAL LANGUAGE

More than 200 translators have already participated in the World Children's Book. Sometimes the research took months, "I had to look for a Tibetan translator for almost a year," says Winterberg. The book is now also available in thousands of language combinations, such as Arabic-Tagalog or Portuguese-Tigrinya — a language spoken in Ethiopia and Eritrea, whose script is reminiscent of children's drawings.

In the years and decades to come the World Children's Book project will continue to grow. The aim is to gradually translate *Am I small?* into over 500 languages.

Many thanks to all readers!

sono piccola?
Ego sum parva?

INTERNATIONAL SUCCESS · OVER 250.000 READERS · WORLDWIDE

MÜNSTER:
VIELFALT MACHEN!

Weltkinderbuch
„Bin ich klein?"

Idee: Philipp Winterberg

ausgezeichnet im Wettbewerb

GUTES
MORGEN
MÜNSTER

About the Author...

Philipp B. Winterberg M.A. studied Communication Science, Psychology and Law. He lives in Berlin and loves being multifaceted: He went parachuting in Namibia, meditated in Thailand, and swam with sharks and stingrays in Fiji and Polynesia.

Philipp Winterberg's books introduce new perspectives on essential themes like friendship, mindfulness and happiness. They are read in languages and countries all over the globe.

Am I small?
わたし、ちいさい？

Five Meters of Time

THE SAFEST PLACE IN THE WORLD
L'ENDROIT LE PLUS SÛR AU MONDE

■ MORE ■ MÁS ■ DI PIÙ ■ PLUS ■ MEHR ■
WWW.PHILIPPWINTERBERG.COM

Namibia
Highlights & Impressions

South Asia
Highlights & Impressions

Highlights & Impressions

billi – ich lese zweisprachig!

WIE PAPA
JUST LIKE DAD

埃格伯特满脸通红

DRÖLF!
Eine Schafgeschichte

Philipp Winterberg Lena Hesse

IN HERE **OUT THERE**

Printed in Great Britain
by Amazon

62782021R00024